Lumi Finds Her Light

An inspiring story about being YOU!

Sandy Parker

MW01140145

All rights reserved. No part of this book may be used or reproduced by any means, graphic, electronic, or mechanical, including photocopying, recording, taping or by any information storage retrieval system without the written permission of the author except in the case of brief quotations embodied in critical articles and reviews.

This is a work of fiction. All of the characters, names, incidents, organizations, and dialogue in this novel are either the products of the author's imagination or are used fictitiously.

Balboa Press books may be ordered through booksellers or by contacting:

Balboa Press
A Division of Hay House
1663 Liberty Drive
Bloomington, IN 47403
www.balboapress.com
1 (877) 407-4847

Because of the dynamic nature of the Internet, any web addresses or links contained in this book may have changed since publication and may no longer be valid. The views expressed in this work are solely those of the author and do not necessarily reflect the views of the publisher, and the publisher hereby disclaims any responsibility for them.

Any people depicted in stock imagery provided by Thinkstock are models, and such images are being used for illustrative purposes only.
Certain stock imagery © Thinkstock.

ISBN: 978-1-5043-5401-1 (sc)
ISBN: 978-1-5043-5407-3 (e)

Library of Congress Control Number: 2016904982

Print information available on the last page.

Balboa Press rev. date: 06/16/2016

PRESS
A DIVISION OF HAY HOUSE

At the end of the day there is a gentle time.
The sun fades to dark and the sky turns to ink.
The stars come out and wink, wink, wink.

It's time for some magic
and soon you'll know it...

when you see the flying creatures
come out to play and show it.

It's not a reflection.
They make their own light.
And you can only see them
when they come out at night.

What are these dots
jumping from the ground to the sky?
They are tiny little lightening bugs
and they love to jump and fly.

Some blink together.
Some shine alone.
And sometimes
they all shine together as one.

Look close and meet Lumi.
She's a lightening bug too.
But her tail won't light up
and she doesn't know what to do.

Lumi wants to light up
so she tries really hard.
She learns and she studies,
even lifts little twigs in the yard.

She watched her friends and tried hard to be like them.
She did what they did but her light was still dim.

One day all this thinking made Lumi feel sad.
It was one of the worst feelings she'd ever had.

Lumi told her Mommy,
"I'm not good like the others
because my light doesn't shine."
Her Mommy said,
"Don't ever believe that!
You will ... at just the right time."

"Lumi, you are not the others
and they are not you.
You will do things the others won't do.
You are perfect. Your light is inside you.
At just the right time, you will shine too."

Lumi kept thinking, "Maybe I am too small.
Maybe I won't shine until I'm more tall."

She thought all the time about these kinds of things.
"Oh, maybe I need to stretch out my wings."

She waited to grow bigger
and she tried to grow more.

She wiggled her tail
while counting to four.

Lumi said to her Mommy, "I wish I were a dolphin. They are sparkly and shine with the water twinkles.

They jump and they dive and see things down deep. It would be better if I were a dolphin, don't you think?"

Lumi's Mommy smiled,
"Dolphins are wonderful
but they are not you.
You will do things
the dolphins don't do.

You are perfect and, Lumi,
the light is inside you.
At just the right time,
your light will shine too."

Lumi wasn't patient
but she tried to be good.
She did all the chores
like a good bug would.

She waited with hope
for her light to shine bright
and dreamed what it would be like
to light up the night.

One day Lumi had an idea
that she thought was so good.
She said to her Mommy,
"I wish I was a bird."

"Their feathers,
they shine with such
glimmers of light.
Birds can see things
way up high when
they are in flight.

It would be better if I was a bird.
Oh Mommy, why?"
But Mommy looked
at her Lumi and sighed.

"Ahh ... no my sweet Lumi,"
said her Mommy wanting so to be heard.
Be proud little Lumi.
You are not a bird.

Birds are fine creatures
but they are not you.
You will do things the birds cannot do.
Your light is inside you.
Your light will shine too.
You are perfect as you are.
Only you can be you."

Days went by and
Lumi started to
think,
"I'll just sit here and
do nothing
until my tail
starts to blink.

I don't fit as a
lightening bug
because I don't
shine.
Everybody knows it –
I'll just wait for my
time."

"Sitting and waiting isn't what we should do,"
Lumi's Mommy told Lumi,
"It can make you feel blue."

Mommies know things and her Mommy was smart.
Mommies think with their senses
and feel with their heart.

"It's time to do something different and new!
Lumi, there is a game I want to play with you.

I will think of a thing that I want you to find
and off we will go into fun play time."

Her Mommy said, "Lumi, look around at this world
and forget being sad.
Let's see what we find that will make us be glad."

"See what happens when we open our eyes.
My sweet little Lumi, you're in for a surprise!"

Lumi slowed down her wings and
went close to the lake.
She looked down and saw a pebble
dancing in the wake.

Lumi flapped her wings and lifted up in the breeze.
She saw a friendly leaf waving hello up in the trees.

Lumi flew lower, way down to the ground. She almost collided with a caterpillar crawling around.

She had to swirl up fast in order to miss him or else she was so close, she might have had to kiss him!

She spun
up quickly and
used her tail to
make a circle.

She got past the
caterpillar ... and oh,
what a miracle!

"My tail, my tail,
it lit up for a
minute!"

Lumi shouted
with joy,
"This is a great
moment
and I'm in it!"

"Yes, Lumi, that's wonderful! Of course your light sparked.

You are a lightening bug and your light should shine in the dark. You are perfect and your light was always going to shine.

But you, my Lumi, had to give it some time."

Lumi waited to see if it would happen again
so she circled her Mommy with the biggest of grins.
Lumi was so happy that she danced and she swirled
and her light lit up again and again in her new
magical world!

Just like Lumi,
you have an inner light.
But you can't be Lumi. In fact,
you're much more bright.

"You are not Lumi
and Lumi is not you.
You will do things
that Lumi won't do.
You are perfect and
your light is inside you.
At just the right time
your light will
shine too."